Welcome to the Forest, where
THE MINISTRY OF MONSTERS
helps humans and monsters live side
by side in peace and harmony...

CONNOR O'GOYLE
lives here too, with his gargoyle mum,
human dad and his dog, Trixie.
But Connor's no ordinary boy...

When monsters get out of control,
Connor's the one for the job.
He's half-monster, he's the Ministry's
NUMBER ONE AGENT,
and he's licensed to do things
no one else can do. He's...

MONSTER BOY!

For Bobby

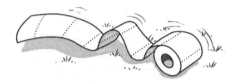

First published in 2009 by Orchard Books
First paperback publication in 2010

ORCHARD BOOKS
338 Euston Road, London NW1 3BH
Orchard Books Australia
Level 17/207 Kent St, Sydney, NSW 2000

ISBN 978 1 40830 241 5 (hardback)
ISBN 978 1 40830 249 1 (paperback)

1 3 5 7 9 10 8 6 4 2 (hardback)
1 3 5 7 9 10 8 6 4 2 (paperback)

Printed in Great Britain

Orchard Books is a division of Hachette Children's Books,
an Hachette UK company.

www.hachette.co.uk

MONSTER BOY

MUMMY MENACE

SHOO RAYNER

ORCHARD BOOKS

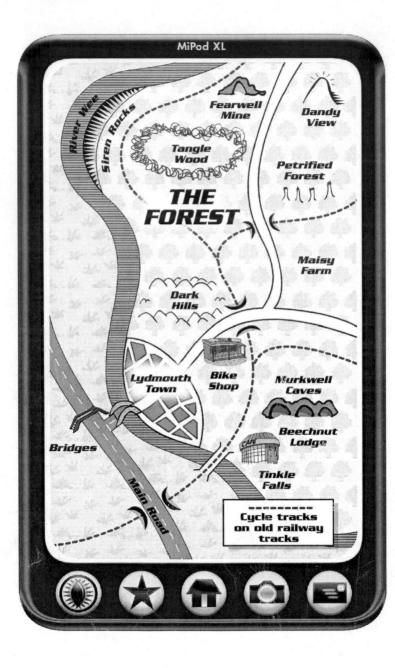

"That's disgusting!"
Connor gasped.

Trixie had
found a toilet roll
in the bushes.
She was playing
with it like a toy.

"You don't know where it's been or where it's come from," Connor called to his dog. "It's probably full of germs!"

Trixie didn't mind.
She was having fun.
It was only a toilet roll!

As she tossed it in the air, the end came loose and began to unwind. She was soon tangled up in the paper.

It was too late. Trixie flapped her wings and swooped around Connor's head. The toilet paper streamed behind her like a ribbon, creating pretty shapes in the air.

Connor sighed and sat down
on a tree stump. There was
nothing to do but wait. Trixie
was having a wonderful time.

Connor's MiPod beeped in his
pocket. It was a message from the
Ministry of Monsters.

MISSION ALERT!

To: Monster Boy,
Number One Agent

From: Mission Control,
Ministry of Monsters

Subject: Someone or something has been taking all the paper from our public toilets.

Suspicious activity has been reported near the loos at the Tinkle Falls Café.

Please investigate immediately.

Good luck!

M.O.M.

THIS MESSAGE WILL SELF-ERASE IN FIFTEEN SECONDS

"I've got a job!" Connor told his mum, as he rushed into the Pedal-O bike shop where they lived. "I'll need MB1 and lots of sandwiches."

Mum pressed a button to open the hidden workshop where she looked after Connor's top-secret Monster Bikes. MB1 was his all-purpose patrol bike.

Five minutes later, Connor was ready and Mum had checked MB1 over.

"All systems are working fine and I've packed orange juice and sandwiches," she said.

"Thanks, Mum." Connor swung his leg over the seat and lifted Trixie into her basket.

Mum gave Connor a little hug. "Please be careful," she said. "I do worry about you!"

"Oh, *Mum!*" Connor groaned, as he pedalled off. "I'll be fine. Stop worrying."

Connor's mum was a Gargoyle, so Connor was half-monster. His code-name was Monster Boy. If anyone could look after himself, Connor could.

Tinkle Falls was a tiny waterfall in the gently flowing River Wee. It was a favourite place for picnickers, with a small café, a children's play area and public toilets.

Connor leant MB1 against a tree and switched on the Monster Detector. Then he sat down on the grass and began to eat his sandwiches.

From behind his sunglasses he surveyed the scene and tried to look like any other kid.

Suddenly, someone screamed. Someone else shouted.

A moving mountain of toilet rolls ran from the toilets and stumbled off into the woods.

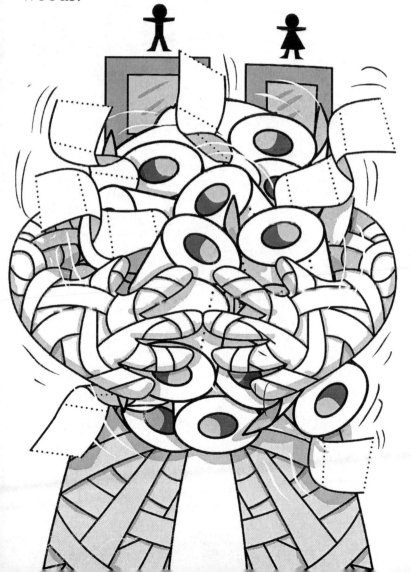

A red light flashed on MB1's control panel.

"Monster alert!" he told Trixie. "Let's get going."

Connor's MiPod pinged again. It was a message from his dad, Gary O'Goyle, the world-famous Mountain Bike Champion. His dad always sent messages at the most unhelpful times!

Hi son,

Having a great time in Egypt at the
Valley of the Kings International
Mountain Bike Championships. There
are no mountains. We have to ride
up and down the pyramids instead!

Lots of love,
Dad

"The pyramids!" Connor muttered under his breath. Suddenly, he had an idea of what he might be dealing with.

Connor leapt onto MB1 and raced off into the woods.

Trixie barked from her basket and pointed her nose at something on the ground. Trixie loved chasing monsters.

"Toilet paper!" Connor whispered. "Well done, Trix. We're on the right track."

It was dark in the woods. Connor switched on the night-vision camera. He turned the handlebar to and fro. A trail of white sheets glowed on the control-panel screen.

"This way," Connor said. Now and then, he caught a glimpse of the monster as they followed the trail of paper through the woods.

Trixie growled. Her fur stood up on end. Connor knew what that meant. The monster must be close.

Connor switched the camera to Monster-Detector vision. The glowing outline of a body showed up on the screen.

"He's just behind that bush," Connor whispered.

Connor pedalled MB1 up to full speed. He raced across the clearing, expertly threw the bike into a half-brake slide and skidded around the back of the bush, taking the monster by surprise.

"Wah!" The monster
leapt into the air,
tossing toilet paper
in all directions.

A dusty cloud of fluttery objects flew into Connor's face. He couldn't breathe. He took his hands off the brakes to brush away the crawling, clinging things.

The bike wobbled. Connor lost his balance. He never saw the tree. He fell off MB1 with a bump!

There was a loud bang, then a hiss as the bike's rescue-beacon balloon filled with gas and floated upwards on its cord. The contents of the first-aid kit spilt out on the ground.

MONSTER BIKE INFO

MB1

MB1 is fitted out with everything that Connor might need on a long Monster Mission.

Control Panel

Monster Detectors

Sandwiches and first-aid box in equipment bays

The ESPxl Monster-Dectector screen can even identify monsters in the dark!

MB1 boasts nine plasma detectors giving it a huge range of 150 metres

Connor squinted through the pain. "I knew it!" he yelped. "You're a Mummy. Why have you been stealing toilet paper?"

"Moths," said the Mummy.

"Moths?!"
Connor squeaked.

"They've been eating my bandages,"
the Mummy explained. "I can't be seen
in public looking like this!"

Connor screwed up his eyes and took a good look at the Mummy. His bandages were chewed to bits. Maggots crawled among the tattered remains. The Mummy was right – he looked terrible.

"You frightened my moths," the Mummy continued. "That's why they flew in your face."

Connor spat a moth from his mouth. "Eugh! But why did you steal the toilet paper?" he asked.

"It's all I could get to patch myself up,"
the Mummy told him. "I've tried
electrical tape, sellotape, even police
crime-scenc tape. The moths chew
through everything. I wish I could get
nice bandages like this."

Connor realised that the Mummy was
gently strapping his leg with the
bandage from the first-aid kit.

"You'll be OK," said the Mummy,
"but it might be sore for a while."

In the distance, Connor heard the
sound of an ambulance responding to
his emergency beacon. He knew he
would be safe now.

MiPOD MONSTER IDENTIFIER PROGRAM

Monster:

Mummy

Distinguishing Features:
Fingers and toes are tied on in case they break and fall off!

Preferred Habitat:
Secret passages and triangular buildings.

Essential Information:
Mummies are not very clever. Most of their brains were scooped out of their noses. The ancient Egyptians did not have toilet paper. They probably used a wet sponge on a stick or a seashell as a scraper!

Danger Rating: 1

Six weeks later, Mum rode Connor to the hospital in the back of the trailer bike. Connor's leg had mended. It was time to have the plaster taken off.

A tall figure loomed in the waiting-room door and called their names.

It was the Mummy! His bandages were clean and fresh and perfectly wrapped.

In the treatment room, the Mummy began gently and carefully cutting off Connor's plaster.

"I should thank you for saving my son's life!" Mum gushed.

The Mummy smiled. "Oh, I only looked after Connor until the ambulance came. It's my fault he had the accident in the first place. Anyway, I have to thank Connor for saving me!"

Mum raised an eyebrow and looked at Connor.

"I told the doctors about the Mummy when they set my leg in plaster," Connor explained. "They were really impressed with his bandaging and offered him a job."

"I hope they pay you properly," Mum said. "People take monsters for granted, you know."

The Mummy smiled.
"They pay me very
well. I get fresh
bandages every week
and a spray to keep
the moths and
maggots away. It's
wonderful – now I can
help people instead of
scaring them and
stealing their
toilet paper."

"A perfect monster solution,"
Connor smiled happily. "But I've
one more question to ask."

"You can ask me anything you like,"
said the Mummy.

Connor looked desperate. "Where's the toilet?"

SHOO RAYNER
MONSTER BOY

All priced at £8.99

The Monster Boy stories are available from all good bookshops,
or can be ordered direct from the publisher:
Orchard Books, PO BOX 29, Douglas IM99 1BQ
Credit card orders please telephone 01624 836000
or fax 01624 837033 or visit our website: www.orchardbooks.co.uk
or e-mail: bookshop@enterprise.net for details.

To order please quote title, author and ISBN
and your full name and address.
Cheques and postal orders should be made payable to 'Bookpost plc.'
Postage and packing is FREE within the UK
(overseas customers should add £2.00 per book).

Prices and availability are subject to change.